SADDLEBACK Classics

Jane Eyre

CHARLOTTE BRONTË

ADAPTED BY

Janice Greene

SADDLEBACK PUBLISHING, INC.

SADDLEBACK *Classics*

The Adventures of Tom Sawyer
Dr. Jekyll and Mr. Hyde
Dracula
Great Expectations
Jane Eyre
Moby Dick
Robinson Crusoe
The Time Machine

Development and Production: Laurel Associates, Inc.
Cover and Interior Art: Black Eagle Productions

SADDLEBACK PUBLISHING, INC.
3505 Cadillac Ave., Building F-9
Costa Mesa, CA 92626-1443

ISBN 1-56254-268-0

Printed in the United States of America
03 02 01 00 M 99   9 8 7 6 5 4 3 2 1

CONTENTS

1 Leaving Gateshead Hall

It was too rainy for a walk that day. The Reed children were all in the drawing room, sitting by the fire. I was alone in another room, looking at a picture book.

I sat in the window seat, hoping that no one would disturb me, when John Reed rudely barged in. He looked about the room and said, "Where in the dickens is Jane? Eliza! Georgiana! Tell Mama that Jane must have run out into the rain—bad animal!"

"She's in the window seat," Eliza said.

I came out immediately, for I trembled at the idea of being dragged out by John.

John Reed was 14—four years older than I. He was large for his age and a bully. I shrank every time he came near me.

"What do you want?" I asked.

"You must say, 'What do you want,

Master Reed,'" he sneered. "You have no business to take our books. You are a *dependent*! Your father left you no money. You ought to beg, and not live here with us. Now, I'll teach you to rummage my book shelves, for they are mine. *All* the house belongs to me—or will in a few years. Go stand by the door!"

I did so. Then I saw him lift the book. I turned aside, but not quickly enough. When the heavy book struck me, my head cracked against the door. The cut bled and the pain was sharp—but now my fear of John was replaced by anger.

"Wicked and cruel boy!" I cried.

He rushed for me, grasping my hair and shoulder. I was frantic. When I pushed him away, he yelled out loud.

Mrs. Reed and Bessie, the maid, came in.

"Dear! What a fury to fly at Master John!" Mrs. Reed said. "Take her away to the red room, Bessie, and lock her in."

As Bessie took me upstairs to the red room, she whispered, "Try to be pleasant, Jane, or she will send you to the poorhouse."

Then she locked the door. The room was dim, with a deep red carpet and curtains. It was here that Mr. Reed had died nine years ago.

I could not remember Mr. Reed, but I knew he was my own uncle—my mother's brother. When my parents had died, he had brought me here to Gateshead Hall. In his last moments before death, he had made Mrs. Reed promise she would raise me as one of her own children. Mrs. Reed probably felt she had kept that promise.

In my terror, a strange idea came to me. I wondered if Mr. Reed's ghost was troubled by the way I was being treated.

Then I thought I saw a ghostly gleam of light on the wall. I screamed and ran to the door. I shook the lock desperately.

Mrs. Reed looked in. "You cannot get out of there with such tricks, Jane! Now you will stay an hour longer!"

"Oh aunt, have pity!" I cried. "Forgive me! I cannot bear it!"

"Silence!" commanded Mrs. Reed. In her eyes, my fear was nothing more than an act.

She pushed me back into the room even

though I was sobbing wildly. I suppose I then had some sort of fit. I fell unconscious.

The next thing I remember is waking in my own bed. A gentleman was bending over me and asking, "Well, who am I?"

I answered that he was Mr. Lloyd, the apothecary. I knew that Mrs. Reed sometimes called him when the servants were ill.

"What made you ill?" Mr. Lloyd asked.

"I was shut up alone in a room where there was a ghost," I said. Then I went on to tell Mr. Lloyd how unhappy I was at Gateshead.

"This child should have a change of scene," Mr. Lloyd said to himself.

Some months later, Mrs. Reed sent for me. A tall man in black was with her in the drawing room. He was straight as a pillar, with a face as stiff as a carved mask.

"This is the little girl I wrote to you about," Mrs. Reed said to him.

"Well, Jane Eyre, are you a good child?" the man asked sternly.

I could not answer yes. Everyone told me I was bad. So I said nothing.

Mrs. Reed said, "Perhaps the less said on

that subject the better, Mr. Brocklehurst."

"There is no sight so sad as that of a naughty child," Mr. Brocklehurst sighed. "Do you know where the wicked go after death?"

"They go to hell," I answered.

"And what must you do to keep from going to hell?" Mr. Brocklehurst asked.

"I must keep in good health and not die," I answered.

Mr. Brocklehurst frowned. "That proves you have a wicked heart. You must pray to God to give you a new and clean one."

"If you accept her at Lowood School, Mr. Brocklehurst, the teachers must keep a close eye on her," Mrs. Reed said. "Above all, you must guard her from her worst fault: The girl is a liar."

"Lying is a sad fault," Mr. Brocklehurst said. "She shall be watched, Mrs. Reed. I will speak to Miss Temple about her."

I wiped the tears from my eyes. Now I would forever be a wicked child in Mr. Brocklehurst's eyes. I would have no chance to prove myself otherwise. Mrs. Reed had crushed any hopes I had for the future.

Mr. Brocklehurst soon left.

"I shall never call you aunt again as long as I live!" I cried out to Mrs. Reed. "You have treated me with miserable cruelty!"

"How dare you say that!" she cried.

I went on in a voice I could not control: "Because it is the *truth*! You think I have no feelings, that I can do without one bit of love or kindness. But I cannot live so. You have no pity. Until my dying day, I shall remember how you locked me in the red room—when I cried out for mercy. You have fooled people into thinking you are a good woman. But you are bad! *You* are a liar!"

Speechless, Mrs. Reed got up and quickly left the room. I was left there alone—winner of the field. For the first time, I tasted something like vengeance. At first the taste was like wine. But its after-flavor was like metal. Somehow I felt as if I had been poisoned.

A few days afterward, on the 19th of January, I left Gateshead Hall.

2 Early Days at Lowood

After a long journey, I arrived at Lowood School. It was late in the evening when I was brought to the dormitory. It was lined with small beds. Surrounded by silence, I fell asleep.

The next morning I woke to a loud bell. I got up reluctantly, for it was bitter cold.

After prayers, we were led into a room for breakfast. Although I was very hungry, the smell of the food was far from inviting. I heard one of the girls say, "*Disgusting!* The porridge is burnt again!" I ate as much as I could, which was very little.

I looked at the girls seated around me. There were about 80 of them, aged from 9 to 20. They were dressed in plain brown dresses and country-made shoes. Their hair was combed straight back from their faces.

Everyone stood up when a tall woman

entered. She had a stately air and was fashionably dressed. I later learned she was Miss Temple, the superintendent of Lowood.

"This morning you had a breakfast which you could not eat. I have ordered that a lunch of bread and cheese shall be served to all."

The teachers looked at her with surprise.

"This is to be done on *my* responsibility," she added in a firm voice.

Soon the bread and cheese were passed out, to the delight of everyone. Then an order was given: "To the garden."

We all went outside. The stronger girls ran about playing games, but the smaller, thinner girls huddled together for warmth. I heard some of them coughing.

I stood by myself, puzzling over some words carved on a nearby stone: *Lowood Institution*. Near me, someone coughed. On a bench close by, an older girl sat reading.

"Can you tell me why they call Lowood an *institution*?" I asked her.

"It is a charity school," she said. "The girls here have lost one or both parents."

"Are you happy here?" I asked.

"You ask too many questions," she said. Later I learned the girl's name was Helen Burns. She seemed a bright pupil. But she was constantly punished for being sloppy.

My first quarter at Lowood seemed to last an age. It was not a golden age, either. I struggled with new rules and new subjects to learn. And life at Lowood was harsh. It was an hour's walk to church every day. We had no boots, so the snow melted in our shoes. My feet became inflamed. It became a torture to put my raw, swollen toes into my shoes in the morning.

One day, after my third week at Lowood, Mr. Brocklehurst came to visit.

When he arrived, we were all in the schoolroom. He quickly walked up to Miss Temple and said, "In settling the accounts, I find that an extra lunch of bread and cheese was served to the girls. How is this?"

Miss Temple said, "I must be responsible for that, sir. The breakfast was so badly cooked the girls could not eat it."

"Madame," said Mr. Brocklehurst sourly, "these girls are not to become used to luxury. Let them remember the sufferings of the Christian martyrs. If you feed their bodies, you are starving their souls!"

Miss Temple's face remained as cold and unmoving as a statue.

As I watched them stare at each other, my slate slipped from my hand and crashed to the floor.

"A careless girl," said Mr. Brocklehurst. "Ah, it is the new girl, I see. Come forward!"

He made me stand up on a stool. "Miss Temple, teachers and children," he said, "do you all see this girl? It is my duty to warn you against her. Keep away from her! Shut her out of your games and conversation. Teachers, keep watch! Punish her body to save her soul. For this girl is—a *liar*!"

"Let her stand half an hour longer on that stool," he went on. "Let no one speak to her for the remainder of the day."

At 5:00 P.M., class was over. When I was left alone, I wept.

After a while, Helen came and comforted me. Then Miss Temple joined us. She took Helen and me to her apartment and gave us

comfortable seats near the warm fire.

"Well, Jane," she said, "an accused criminal is always allowed to speak in his defense. You have been accused of lying— defend yourself as well as you can."

I told her the story of my sad childhood, including the terrors I felt when I was locked in the red room. When I had finished, she said, "I know something of Mr. Lloyd. I shall write to him. If his answer agrees with what you have said, you are clear of all accusations. To me, Jane," she said with a friendly smile, "you are clear now."

She then turned to Helen Burns. "How are you tonight, Helen?" she asked kindly. "Have you coughed much today?"

"Not quite so much, ma'am," Helen said.

Miss Temple served tea and generous slices of seed-cake—a feast for us. All too soon the bell rang, and our evening ended.

Miss Temple wrote to Mr. Lloyd. His answer cleared me of guilt. Miss Temple then gathered everyone at the school and announced that I was clear of all charges that had been made against me. The teachers shook hands with me and kissed me.

From that hour I determined to do the best I could. I worked hard, and in a few weeks I was moved to a higher class. In less than two months I was allowed to begin French and drawing lessons.

I became almost happy. Now I would not have traded Lowood, with all its hardships, for Gateshead and its luxuries.

3

A New Position

Gradually, as winter gave way to spring, the hardships of Lowood seemed to lighten. The trees, which had been dark skeletons all winter, now slowly came back to life. Wildflowers popped up everywhere.

I was free to roam outside from sunrise until night. And the cause of my freedom? Typhus had turned the school into a hospital.

Classes were broken up. Rules were relaxed. Girls who were lucky enough to have friends or family went home to them. But many went home to die.

I had not seen Helen for many weeks. She was ill not from typhus, but consumption. I had been ignorant enough to think her illness was mild. One day, however, I finally asked a nurse how she was.

"Poor girl! The doctor says she'll not be

with us long," the nurse explained sadly.

I felt a shock of horror. Somehow I had to see Helen. That night, when the other girls were asleep, I quietly set off for Miss Temple's room, where Helen was staying.

The door was open, but Miss Temple was not there. Helen lay in a small bed. I pulled back the bed curtain and whispered, "Helen! Are you awake?"

"Can it be you, Jane?" she asked in her sweet, gentle voice.

I lay down beside her. "I *had* to see you, Helen! I heard you were very ill."

"Dear Jane!" she said. "You came to bid me goodbye, then."

"Oh, no, Helen!" I turned my head away to hide my tears.

"There is nothing to grieve about, Jane," Helen said. "My mind is at rest. I have faith—I know I am going to God."

I held her close and heard her whisper, "I feel as if I could sleep now. But don't leave me, Jane. I like to have you near me."

"I'll stay with you, Helen. No one shall take me away," I promised.

When I awoke it was day. I was not in Helen's bed, but my own. When Miss Temple had returned to her room she had found me asleep—and Helen was dead.

* * * *

I shall now pass a space of eight years. Only a few lines are necessary to describe the events that happened.

The epidemic of typhus finally ran its course. But the great number of deaths at the school caused a great scandal. An investigation showed the institution was built on damp, unhealthy ground. Also, the food was often prepared in dirty water.

Several wealthy people in the county donated money so that Lowood could be moved to a healthier spot. The girls were given better food and warmer clothes. Mr. Brocklehurst, because of his wealth and family, was still part of the school, but he was much less powerful than before. Now, a committee ran Lowood—with a softer hand. In time, the school became a truly noble institution. I stayed there eight years.

six as a student and two as a teacher.

All this time, Miss Temple had stayed at Lowood. For me she was a mother, a teacher, and as the years went by—a friend. But destiny, in the name of Reverend Mr. Nasmyth, came between me and Miss Temple. He married her, and they moved to a distant county.

From the day she left, I was no longer content. For eight years, my world had been Lowood School. Now I became restless. I longed for change, for liberty.

I advertised in the local newspaper for a position as a governess. After a long week of waiting, I received but one reply. It was from a Mrs. Fairfax at Thornfield Hall. She wished to find a governess for one little girl. I examined the letter a long time. All seemed satisfactory. Yes—to Thornfield I would go.

Since Mrs. Reed was still my guardian, I had to ask her permission to leave. She wrote that I might do as I pleased.

I busied myself in getting ready. The time passed quickly. Then one October morning, my last day at Lowood had arrived. I was waiting for the coach when a servant said that a visitor wished to see me.

A woman who looked like a well-dressed servant was waiting. It was Bessie, Mrs. Reed's kindly maid! I hugged her warmly.

"Did Mrs. Reed send you here, Bessie?" I asked.

"No, dear," Bessie said. "I just wanted to get a last look at you—before you went out of my reach."

I laughed as Bessie looked me over. "Are you disappointed in me?" I asked.

"No, Miss Jane, not exactly," Bessie said. "You look like a lady, as I expected. You were never a beauty, but you will do well."

I smiled at Bessie's frank answer, but in truth I wished I was not quite so plain.

"There was something I wanted to ask you," Bessie said. "Have you ever heard from your father's family, the Eyres?"

"Never in my life," I said.

Bessie said, "One day nearly seven years ago, a Mr. Eyre came to see you. When Mrs. Reed said you were at school 50 miles off, he was disappointed. Quite a gentleman, he

looked. He said he was about to take a voyage to a foreign country—a place where they make wine."

"Madeira?" I suggested.

"Why, yes! That was it!" Bessie said. "I believe he was your father's brother. He didn't stay long at the house."

Bessie and I talked for an hour. Then she set off for Gateshead, and I left for my new life at Thornfield Hall. I prayed that Mrs. Fairfax would not be another Mrs. Reed.

After a long journey, I arrived on a cold

October night. A servant led me into a snug, small room where an elderly lady sat knitting by the fire. It was Mrs. Fairfax. She greeted me kindly, and told a servant to bring me sandwiches and hot negus.

I asked, "Shall I have the pleasure of meeting Miss Fairfax tonight?"

"Miss *Fairfax*?" she said. "Oh, you mean Miss Varens. Varens is the name of your future student. I am only the housekeeper here. Miss Varens is the ward of Mr. Rochester, the master of Thornfield Hall. Mr. Rochester seldom visits us, though.

"I am so glad you have come," Mrs. Fairfax went on. "Thornfield Hall was quite lonely last winter with only Leah and the other servants to talk to. But then little Miss Varens came in the spring. And now that you are here, I shall be quite happy."

My heart warmed to the kind old lady. That night I knelt by my bedside and offered up thanks where thanks were due.

4 A Ghostly Laugh

The next morning, I met my pupil, Adèle, and her nurse, Sophie. Adèle was perhaps seven or eight years old. She had a pale face and curls that fell to her waist. She greeted me in French.

"I wish you would ask her a question or two about her parents," Mrs. Fairfax said. "I wonder if she remembers them?"

I asked Adèle whom she had lived with before she came to England. She said, "I used to live with Mama, but she has gone to the Holy Virgin. She taught me how to sing and dance. Shall I sing for you now?"

She sang a song from an opera. It was about a woman cheated by her lover. I thought it in very bad taste for a small child.

After breakfast, Adèle and I went to the library. This was the room Mr. Rochester had set aside for Adèle's lessons. I found her well behaved, but not accustomed to schoolwork. I let the first day be an easy one.

When the lessons were over, Mrs. Fairfax showed me around Thornfield Hall. She led me through the large front bedrooms of the second floor to the third floor. Over the years, the older pieces of furniture had been moved to this floor. I liked the hush and gloom of these darkened rooms. But I would not have liked to spend a night on one of those wide, heavy beds.

Mrs. Fairfax said, "No one ever sleeps here. One would say that if there was a ghost at Thornfield, this would be its haunt."

"I would agree," I said with a smile. "But you have no ghost, surely?"

Mrs. Fairfax smiled. "None that I ever heard of. Come, Jane—let me show you the view from the roof."

I followed her up a narrow staircase to the attic. Then we climbed a ladder and came out through a trapdoor to the roof.

I leaned over the battlements and viewed the grounds below—the wide field and ancient thorn trees, the church and a ring of hills. All looked peaceful in the autumn sun.

Mrs. Fairfax stayed behind a moment to fasten the trapdoor. I went back down the narrow staircase.

Then I heard the last sound I expected to hear in such a quiet place: a laugh. It was a strange laugh, low and mirthless. It seemed to echo in every room.

"Mrs. Fairfax!" I called out. "Did you hear that laugh? Who is it?"

"One of the servants, I suppose," Mrs. Fairfax said. "Perhaps it was Grace Poole. She sews in one of these rooms."

Then the laugh came again. This time it ended in an odd murmur.

Mrs. Fairfax called out, *"Grace!"*

The door nearest me opened, and a servant came out. She was a big woman of about 40, with a hard, plain face. I could not imagine anyone less ghostly.

"Too much noise, Grace!" Mrs. Fairfax said. "Remember directions."

The servant curtsied and went back into the room. Then Adèle came running up to us, saying that it was time for our dinner.

The following months passed quietly. Mrs. Fairfax turned out to be what she had seemed at first—a gentle woman of average intelligence. Adèle had been a spoiled child before coming to England. But she was eager to please and soon settled down to her studies.

Although my life at Thornfield Hall was pleasant and comfortable, I was restless. Sometimes I would climb up to the trapdoor on the roof and look far out over field and hill. I longed to go farther than I could see—to reach the busy world beyond.

One afternoon in January, I went to the town of Hay to post a letter for Mrs. Fairfax. I walked quickly, for the day was cold. A thin sheet of ice covered the lane. Thornfield was a mile behind me when I heard the sound of a horse coming. Next a black and white dog, with long hair and a huge head, ran by me, followed by a rider on a tall horse. Then a moment later, I heard a sliding sound, a tumble, and a thud. The horse had slipped on the ice!

I hurried down to where the man and his

horse were struggling to rise. The dog circled them, barking loudly.

"Are you injured, sir?" I asked.

"Stand out of the way!" the man snapped.

The horse got up on its feet. The man stood, too, then limped to a stone wall, sat down, and felt his ankle. He silenced the dog with, "Down, Pilot!"

"If you are hurt and want help, sir," I said, "I live just below. Perhaps I can fetch someone from Thornfield Hall."

"Thank you," he said, "but I have no broken bones—only a sprain." He tried to stand, but the pain made him grunt. It was still light enough to see him clearly. He was of middle height, and very broad across the chest. He had a dark face, a stern look, and a heavy brow. I judged him to be about 35.

"You say that you live just below—at Thornfield?" he asked.

"Yes, sir. I was on my way to Hay to post a letter for Mrs. Fairfax."

"Will you help me get on my horse?"

He laid a heavy hand on my shoulder and limped to his horse. Then he sprang to the saddle, biting down on his lip in pain.

"Now go take your letter to Hay," he said, "and return as fast as you can."

I quickly walked to Hay and back to Thornfield Hall. I did not like coming back. I did not wish to sit in my lonely little room, and then pass the evening with only quiet Mrs. Fairfax for company.

At last I went inside. A large black and white dog sat on Mrs. Fairfax's rug.

"Pilot!" I said in surprise. He came up and sniffed my hand.

I rang the bell, for it had grown dark and I needed a candle. When Leah entered I asked her, "Tell me—whose dog is this?"

"It belongs to the master, Mr. Rochester," Leah said. "He has just arrived!"

5 | Mr. Rochester's Return

Thornfield was no longer as silent as a church. For my part, I liked it better. Mr. Rochester's agent soon arrived, and some of his tenants. There were knocks at the door, clangs of bells, footsteps, and new voices. Adèle was not easy to teach that day. Mr. Rochester had hinted that he had brought her a present.

That evening, Mr. Rochester asked Mrs. Fairfax, Adèle, and me to join him for tea in the drawing room. He sat on a couch near the fire, his leg on a cushion.

After tea had been brought in, Adèle asked, "Did you bring a present for Miss Eyre?"

"Did you *expect* a present, Miss Eyre?" he asked gruffly.

Embarrassed, I said, "Not at all, sir. After all, I am but a stranger to you. I have done nothing at all to deserve a present."

He said, "Oh, don't fall back on modesty. I have examined Adèle. She is not bright— yet in the short time you've been here she has made much improvement."

"Sir," I said, "you have now given me my present. All teachers wish to hear such praise for their work."

"Hmmmph!" said Mr. Rochester. He took a sip of tea. "You came here from—?"

"From Lowood School, sir. I was there for eight years."

"*Eight years!*" he said. "Half that many years should have been the end of you. No wonder you have the look of another world.

"Adèle showed me a few of your drawings this afternoon," Mr. Rochester went on. "Did you draw these pictures all by yourself, or did a master help you?"

"No, indeed! The drawings are mine!"

He smiled. "Ah, that pricks your pride, I see. Well, fetch me your portfolio."

I brought the portfolio from the library. He looked carefully at every sketch and painting. At last he said, "For a school girl, the drawings are peculiar. Your ideas are elfish. Those eyes in the Evening Star you must have seen in a dream. And who taught you to paint wind? There—put the drawings away!"

Suddenly, he looked at his watch. "Why, it's nine o'clock, Miss Eyre. What are you thinking, to let Adèle stay up so late? Take her to bed now!"

We left him. "Mr. Rochester seems to be a very changeful and abrupt man," I confided to Mrs. Fairfax.

"It's true," she said. "But I suppose that I have become accustomed to his manner. Mr. Rochester has painful thoughts—no doubt, because of troubles with his family."

"But he has no family," I said.

"Not now, but he once did," said Mrs. Fairfax. "His father and older brother were not quite fair to Mr. Rochester. They caused him a great deal of suffering. I never knew exactly what happened. But for many years now, Mr. Rochester has led an unsettled kind of life. The death of his older brother made him master of Thornfield, but he shuns the place."

"Why should he shun it?" I asked.

"Perhaps he thinks it gloomy," she said. I would have liked a clearer answer. But Mrs. Fairfax could not—or would not—tell me anything more.

I saw little of Mr. Rochester for several days. Then, one night after dinner, he sent for me. He seemed at ease now. There was a smile on his lips and a sparkle in his eye, perhaps from his wine at dinner. As I watched his face, he caught me looking at him.

"You examine me, Miss Eyre," he said. "Do you think me handsome?"

The words slipped from my tongue before I had time to think. "No, sir," I said.

"Ah! By my word!" he laughed. "There *is* something unusual about you. You look so grave and simple. Then you stick a penknife under my ear. What do you mean by it?"

"Sir, I beg your pardon," I replied. "I ought to have said that beauty is of little value, or something of that sort."

"You ought to have replied no such thing!" he laughed. "But tonight it would please me to learn more of *you*. Therefore, speak."

I said nothing.

"I see you are stubborn," he said, "and annoyed. I beg your pardon, Miss Eyre. The fact is, I don't wish to treat you like an inferior. You are frank and sincere. You seem to be cast in a different mold from most people. Of course, I may be reaching my conclusions too quickly. You may have more faults than good points."

"And so may you," I thought to myself.

He answered as if I had spoken out loud. "Yes, you are right. I have many faults of my own. I was pushed on the wrong track at the age of one and twenty. I have never found the right course since. Do you wonder that I tell you this? I can talk to you almost as freely as if I were writing my thoughts in a diary."

Just then Adèle entered. She was wearing her present from Mr. Rochester. It was a lovely dress of rose-colored satin.

She danced across the room to Mr. Rochester and dropped down on one knee at his feet. "Sir, thank you a thousand times for your kindness!" the little girl cried happily. "That is how Mama would have said it. Isn't that right, sir?"

"Pre-cise-ly!" Mr. Rochester laughed. Then he turned to me and said, "And that is how she charmed my English gold out of my British pocket. Good night."

One afternoon, Mr. Rochester told me the story of Adèle's mother, Céline Varens, the opera dancer. She had once been his mistress. "I gave her servants, a carriage, diamonds, cashmeres, and lace," he said. "But she betrayed me with a brainless young officer. Seeing Céline with this worthless young man, my love was instantly snuffed out. Unfortunately, months before, Céline told me that Adèle was my daughter, though I see no resemblance. Indeed, *Pilot* is more like me than she is!"

"Perhaps now that you know Adèle's story," he went on, "you will think differently of her. You will soon beg me to look for a new governess, eh?"

I said, "Oh, no! Adèle is innocent of her mother's faults—and yours. I shall cling closer to her than before."

As the weeks passed, Mr. Rochester told me much about himself and the larger world

I had never seen. I took a keen delight in following him through the new places he described. And now was Mr. Rochester ugly in my eyes? No, reader, his face was the one I liked best to see.

He did have his faults. He was proud and harsh. Often, he was gloomy indeed. I would have done much to lighten his dark moods.

One night, I lay awake, wondering why Mr. Rochester came to Thornfield so seldom. I wondered if he would be leaving again soon. If he did, how joyless Thornfield would be without him!

That night I was startled wide awake on hearing a strange murmur in the hall. I sat up in bed. Just then I heard someone outside my door. The sound was like fingers feeling their way down the hall in the dark.

Fire and Mystery

From the hall I heard a laugh, low and deep, then footsteps heading toward the third-story staircase. It was now impossible to stay by myself! I must hurry to Mrs. Fairfax. I got dressed and stepped into the hall, where I smelled something burning.

The door to Mr. Rochester's room was ajar, and smoke was rushing out. In an instant, I was in the room. Tongues of flame darted round the bed where he slept. The bed curtains were on fire!

"Wake! Wake!" I cried. I shook him, but he only murmured and turned in his bed. The smoke had stupefied him! I rushed to his basin and splashed some water on him.

Mr. Rochester woke at last. "What? Is there a flood?" he cried.

"Your bed curtains are on fire!" I cried,

dousing them with the rest of the water. "There! It's out now. How could such a thing have happened?"

I left him alone to find dry clothes while I brought in a candle.

"Shall I call Mrs. Fairfax?" I asked.

"No," he said. "I am going to leave for a few minutes, Jane. Stay where you are until I return. I must go to the third story."

I waited a very long time in the dark and cold. When at last he came back, I told him of the footsteps, and the eerie laugh—which I thought might be Grace Poole's.

"You must say nothing about this," he said, pointing to the burned curtains. "*I* will account for this state of affairs. Now please return to your own room."

"Good night then, sir," I said coldly.

"What! Why are you leaving me in this way, Jane?" he exclaimed.

"You said I should go, sir."

"But don't go without my thanks!" he said. "Why, you have saved my life!"

He took my hand. "I knew you would do me good in some way," he said. "I saw it in your eyes when I first beheld you. The look in your eyes and the smile on your face struck deep in my heart. . . ."

Then words I could not quite hear trembled on his lips. But he could not speak.

At last he let go of my hand and said, "My dear protector, good night!"

I went back to my room, but never once thought of sleep. Until morning, I was tossed on a restless sea of trouble and joy.

The next morning, I both wished and feared to see Mr. Rochester. But the whole day passed without a glimpse of him.

Grace Poole greeted me in her usual way. I was amazed. Why had she not been turned over to the police?

All day I longed to see Mr. Rochester and ask him about Grace Poole. But that afternoon at tea I learned from Mrs. Fairfax that he had left Thornfield for two weeks. He was joining a large party at a Mr. Eshton's place, several miles away.

"Will there be ladies in the party?" I asked Mrs. Fairfax.

"Oh, yes," she said, "Mrs. Eshton and her

three daughters, very elegant young ladies, will be there, and Blanche and Mary Ingram. I saw Blanche when she came here to a Christmas ball that Mr. Rochester gave. Everyone thought her the most beautiful woman there. She was tall, with a fine bust and a long, graceful neck. Her eyes were like Mr. Rochester's—large and black."

"Then perhaps she is a favorite of Mr. Rochester's?" I asked curiously.

"Oh, I think not," said Mrs. Fairfax. "But, Jane—you eat nothing. Why, you have hardly tasted your food!"

"No, I am too thirsty to eat," I said. "But will you pour me another cup of tea?"

When I was alone, I examined my heart. I sadly decided there was no greater fool than Jane Eyre.

A few weeks later, Mrs. Fairfax received a letter from Mr. Rochester. She said, "He will be coming in three days—and not alone. He is bringing the party with him, so the house must be made ready."

I have never seen such a washing of walls, polishing of mirrors, and beating of carpets. At last, when all was ready, the party arrived. "Mr. Rochester would like Adèle to come to the drawing room after dinner," Mrs. Fairfax told me, "and he would like you to come also."

After dinner, Adèle and I sat waiting in the drawing room. Before long, the guests came in. I rose and curtsied to them. One or two nodded in return. The others only stared.

I looked over the figures before me. Blanche Ingram was indeed as Mrs. Fairfax had described. She was tall and graceful. The dark eyes were beautiful—but her face? It was proud and pompous.

And where was Mr. Rochester? He entered last. I found I could not keep my eyes from him. I tried to hide my feelings, for I know he could not care for me. And yet, while I breathe and think, I must love him.

Now Miss Ingram was asking Mr. Rochester about Adèle. "How did you come to be in charge of such a little doll as that?" she said. "Where did you pick her up?"

Mr. Rochester said, "I did not pick her up, she was left on my hands."

"I suppose you have a governess for her— that person over there," she said. "What a *nuisance* a governess is! But I never suffered much from them. What tricks we used to play on our governesses!"

After a few more minutes on this subject, Miss Ingram insisted that Mr. Rochester sing a song for his guests.

"I am your servant," said Mr. Rochester.

Now is my time to slip away, I thought. But Mr. Rochester's voice stopped me. It was a deep bass voice—rich, mellow, and powerful. I waited until the song had ended, then left the room quietly. How surprised I was when he followed me out.

"You are pale and depressed, Jane," he said. "What troubles you? Tell me!"

"Nothing, sir. I am not depressed."

"But your eyes are full of tears," he said. "Indeed a bead has slipped from a lash and fallen. If I was not afraid of some prig of a servant passing," he continued, "I would find out what all this means. But I excuse you for now. Good night, my . . . " He stopped, bit his lip, and was gone.

# A Vicious Attack

In the days that followed, I watched Miss Ingram and Mr. Rochester. They were always paired in charades. They spent much time in conversation. He was clearly her favorite. I saw him look at her often, yet somehow I felt sure that he did not love her.

But I saw he was going to marry her. Perhaps this was for family—or because of her connections. I supposed this was what people of their class were expected to do.

I was miserable indeed, yet I could not be jealous of Miss Ingram. She was very showy, but she was not quite genuine. Her thoughts were not her own, but parroted from books. And she was not a *good* person; tenderness and truth were not in her. I wondered how she could keep Mr. Rochester happy as his wife.

One day, Mr. Rochester went into town on business. The rest of the party had talked about visiting a gypsy camp nearby. But they had decided that the day was too wet.

In the middle of the afternoon a visitor arrived. Mr. Mason was from the West Indies. He was a tall, handsome man, but his eyes had no spirit. He was warming himself by the fire when a servant announced that one of the gypsies had come to Thornfield Hall. Her name was Mother Bunches, the servant said, and she had come to tell the ladies' fortunes.

"Oh, yes! Yes!" cried the young women. "It will be excellent sport."

Miss Ingram demanded to be the first. She left the room for 15 minutes. When she returned, she was in a sour mood indeed.

I was the last. I went up to the gypsy, who wore a red cloak and a broad black hat that hid her face. She questioned me about Mr. Rochester, and my plans for the future. Then, strangely, her voice changed. She looked up to me and took off her hat.

Then I heard a familiar voice say, "Well, Jane, do you know me?"

"Mr. Rochester!" I cried. "I believe you have been trying to draw me out. Why, that is hardly fair, sir!"

"Do you forgive me, Jane?"

"I cannot tell until I have thought it all over," I said. "But sir—did you know that a Mr. Mason has come to see you?"

Mr. Rochester turned white as ashes. He said, "No, Jane! This is a blow!"

"Can I help you, sir? I'd do anything to serve you."

He said, "Dear Jane! If help is wanted, I'll seek it at your hands, I promise you that."

I brought him a glass of wine. Soon he looked steady and stern again. Sometime later, I heard him say, "This way, Mason. Here is your room." He spoke so cheerfully my heart was at ease. I soon fell asleep.

A bright moon woke me in the dead of night. I rose to pull the bed curtain.

Then the silence of the night was torn by a sharp scream. Good God, what a cry!

Now I heard a struggle. It was in the room just above mine. A voice cried, "Rochester! Rochester! For God's sake, *hurry!*"

I put on some clothes and ran from my room. The hall was filled with frightened guests. Mr. Rochester soon walked in with a candle. "All is well!" he cried. "A servant has had a nightmare. That is all. Now please go back to your rooms or you will take cold."

I returned to my room, but not to my bed. I was sure that more had happened than Mr. Rochester had told his guests. I wanted to be ready for emergencies. Before long, there was a quiet tap on my door.

"Am I wanted?" I asked.

Mr. Rochester whispered, "Have you a sponge in your room? And volatile salts?"

"Yes," I answered.

"Follow me then, and make no noise."

He led me to the third story. We went into a room that Mrs. Fairfax had once shown me. A tapestry was now looped over a door that had been hidden behind it. Just beyond the door I heard a snarling sound, almost like a dog. Then a shout of laughter—*Grace Poole!*

On the other side of the bed Mr. Mason sat in a chair, his head leaning back. One of his sleeves was soaked in blood.

"Jane," said Mr. Rochester, "I am going to fetch the doctor. Put the sponge to his wound when he bleeds. Give him the salts if he feels faint. You must not speak to him."

Then he spoke to Mr. Mason. "Richard, not one word will you say to her—at the peril of your life."

When he left the room, I was left alone with the pale and bloody man. This I was able to bear. But the thought of Grace Poole bursting out at me made me shudder.

Later, as the first gray streaks of dawn appeared at the window, I heard Pilot barking below. Then at last Mr. Rochester entered with Dr. Carter.

The doctor frowned as he examined Mr. Mason's wound. "How is this?" he said. "The flesh is torn as well as cut."

"She bit me like a tiger," Mr. Mason said. "Then Rochester grabbed the knife. I did not expect it. She was so quiet at first."

"I warned you," said Mr. Rochester. "It was folly to see her alone."

"She sucked the blood and said she'd drain my heart!" Mr. Mason cried in horror.

Mr. Rochester looked pained. "Come, be silent, Richard!" he said. "Don't repeat her meaningless gibberish."

At half past five, Mr. Rochester and Dr. Carter helped Mr. Mason into a waiting carriage. Lifting his head to Mr. Rochester, Mr. Mason said, "Let her be taken care of. Let her be treated tenderly. Let her . . . " Then he stopped speaking and burst into tears.

"I do my best," said Mr. Rochester.

"Will Grace Poole live here still, sir?" I asked when the carriage had left.

"Oh, yes, Jane!" he answered, "but don't trouble your head about her."

"Yet it seems your life is hardly secure while she stays," I said.

"Never fear, I can take care of myself," he said. "You were a great help to me last night. You *are* my little friend, are you not?"

"I like to serve you, sir," I said. "I want to obey you in all that is right."

He said, "Exactly! I see you are truly happy when you are pleasing me—when you are doing *all that is right*. But if I asked you to do wrong, there would be no light foot running to help. My friend would then turn to me, quiet and pale. She would say, 'No, sir, that is impossible.' You would be as unchangeable as a fixed star.

"Well, you too have power over me, Jane. For that reason you may injure me. So I dare not show you my weaknesses."

Suddenly his voice changed, becoming harsh and sarcastic. "You have noticed my tender feelings for Miss Ingram, have you not? Will you promise to sit up with me the night before I am married? I am sure I shall not be able to sleep."

"Yes, sir," I said with a sinking heart.

He then waved to two of his guests who were walking by the stables. Leaving me, he greeted them cheerfully, saying, "Mason had to leave early this morning. He was gone before sunrise. I rose at four to see him off."

Return to Gateshead

The next morning, I was surprised to hear I had a visitor. It was Bessie's husband, Robert, just arrived from Gateshead. He was dressed all in black: John Reed was dead.

"His life had been very wild," Robert said. "He got into debt and then into jail. His mother helped him out twice, but then he returned to his old ways. How he died, God knows! They say he killed himself."

I was silent. The news was frightful.

"Mrs. Reed has not been well these last few years," Robert went on. "The news of Mr. John's death brought on a stroke. She has been asking for you, Miss Eyre."

Immediately, I went in search of Mr. Rochester to tell him that I must leave.

"Promise to stay only a week," he said.

"I had better not give my word," I said.

"I might have to break it. And sir, you have as good as told me that you are going to be married. In that case, you must arrange for Adèle to go away to school."

"And you?"

"I must advertise for another place, sir."

"Of course!" he exclaimed, with a sad look clouding his face. "But promise not to advertise just yet. Trust this to me."

"I shall be glad to do so," I answered, "if you will promise that Adèle and Mrs. Fairfax shall both be safely out of the house before your bride enters it."

"Very well! You go tomorrow then?"

"Yes, sir—early."

I reached Gateshead on the first of May. The house looked much the same, but the people in it had changed so much that I hardly recognized them.

Miss Eliza was tall, thin, and now had a severe-looking face. Miss Georgiana was plump and fair and pretty. Though they both wore black, Georgiana's dress looked stylish, while Eliza's gave her the air of a nun.

They greeted me coolly, and said their

mother was too tired to see me that night.

Their rudeness did not have the power over me it once had. "If you would just step upstairs and tell her I have come," I insisted, "I should be much obliged to you."

A few moments later I was at her side. Although I had once vowed that I would never call her aunt again, it now seemed no sin to break that vow.

"How are you, dear aunt?" I asked.

"Is it Jane Eyre?" she asked.

"Yes, I am Jane Eyre," I said.

"I have had more trouble with that child than anyone would believe. I could not understand her. I declare she once talked to me like a mad person—no child ever looked or spoke as she did. So many of the pupils died at Lowood. I wish *she* had died!"

"A strange wish, Mrs. Reed," I said calmly. "Why did you hate her so?"

"I always had a dislike for her mother. She was my husband's favorite. When she died, he wept like a simpleton and made me keep the baby. He wanted our children to be friendly to the little beggar. In his last illness, he made me vow to keep her. My husband was weak—always weak! John is not at all like his father. But oh, how I wish he would stop writing me for money!"

I quickly left her then, as she was becoming excited. It was several days later before I spoke with her again. When I looked into her face, she said weakly, "Today I cannot even move a limb. It is well that I should ease my mind before I die. Are we alone?"

"Yes," I said.

"Jane, I have twice done you a wrong for which I am sorry now. One was in breaking my promise to my husband that I would bring you up as my own child. The other—" she stopped and looked away.

A few moments later, she went on, "Well, I must get over it. Eternity is before me. Go to my dresser, Jane. There is a letter inside. Find it and read it aloud."

Madam,
Will you have the goodness to send
me the address of my niece, Jane Eyre,

and tell me if she is well? It is my intention to invite her to come to Madeira. As I am unmarried and have no children, I wish to adopt her, and leave her all I have when I die.

John Eyre.

A letter from my uncle! It was dated more than three years ago.

"Why did I never hear of this?" I asked.

"I disliked you too much to help you," she admitted. "I can never forget the day that you flew at me in such a fury."

"Dear aunt, forgive me," I said. "Please remember that I was but a child then."

"I tell you I never forgot that day. So I took my revenge. I wrote to your uncle and told him you had died of typhus at Lowood. Now you must act as you please. Write and tell him I lied. You were born, I think, to be my torment. Even my last hour is tortured by the memory of my bad deed."

I tried to comfort her. "Please think no more of it now. You have my full and free forgiveness. Kiss me, aunt."

I brought my cheek close to her lips, but she would not touch it. Poor, miserable woman! Living, she had forever hated me. Dying, she hated me still.

Soon after, she fell into a stupor. At midnight, she died.

To help settle the family's affairs, I stayed at Gateshead a month. I shall not be referring to the sisters again, so I will now mention what became of them. Georgiana made a good match, marrying a wealthy but worn-out man of fashion. Eliza indeed took the veil, and today she is the superior at a convent of nuns in France.

I returned to Thornfield on an evening in June. As I approached the house I felt glad—so glad I had to remind myself I would not be staying long.

Mr. Rochester was alone in the garden. He called out to me, "Hello! There you are, truant! Gone from me a whole month. I'm sure you've quite forgotten me. And how like you not to call a carriage, but to come home as quietly as a dream or a ghost."

He had spoken of Thornfield Hall as if it

were my home! The warmth of his greeting made me speak, in spite of myself. "Mr. Rochester," I said, "for some reason I am strangely glad to come back again to you. It seems that wherever *you* are is my home— my only home."

Then, embarrassed, I turned away from him. I walked so fast he probably could not have caught up with me if he had tried.

# 9 A Shocking Surprise

The next few weeks, nothing was said about Mr. Rochester's wedding to Miss Ingram. For no good reason, I began to hope.

One evening Mr. Rochester and I took a leisurely walk toward the horse chestnut tree. "Thornfield is a pleasant place in the summer, is it not?" he asked. "I believe you have liked living here."

"Yes, indeed, sir," I said.

"I'm sorry, Jane," he said. "In a month I shall be married. But I have heard of another place for you. Your work would be to educate the five daughters of Mrs. Dionysis O'Gall of Bitternutt Lodge, in Ireland."

"That is a long way off, sir," I said.

"From what?" he asked.

"Why, from England and from Thornfield and—" I answered.

"Well?"

"From *you,* sir."

"Then you must stay! I swear it!"

My feelings, stirred by grief and love, broke free at last. "I tell you I must go!" I cried out. "Do you think I can stay here as *nothing* to you? Do you think I am a machine without feelings? Do you think because I am poor and plain that I have no soul and heart? You think wrong! But if God had given me beauty and wealth, I swear I would have made it as hard for you to leave me as it is now for me to leave you. I am not talking to you of customs, or even of mortal flesh. It is my spirit that speaks to your spirit, as if we stood at God's feet—*equal!*"

"Equal!" repeated Mr. Rochester. He drew me to his chest and kissed me.

"Equal, and yet not equal," I said. "For you are as good as married—and to a woman you do not truly love! I would scorn such a marriage. Therefore, I am better than you. I have spoken my mind, and now I shall go."

"Jane, be still. Don't struggle so. You are like a wild, frantic little bird, tearing at its own feathers in order to be free."

"I am no bird. I am a free human being—free to leave *you*."

I tore myself from his arms. "But Jane, I call you as my wife," he cried. "It is only *you* I wish to marry."

I was silent. I thought he mocked me.

His voice then became passionate. "I would not—*could* not—marry Miss Ingram," he said. "You, you strange, almost unearthly thing! I love you as my own flesh. You, poor and plain and small as you are, I beg you to accept me as your husband."

"Then, sir, I will marry you."

"Let me hold you, Jane," he said in his deepest tone. "Come to me now."

What had become of the calm evening? The wind roared in the walk. It was so dark I could hardly see Mr. Rochester's face. Then a bright spark leapt out of a cloud. There was a crash of lightning and I hid my dazzled eyes against Mr. Rochester's shoulder. The rain poured down.

That night Mr. Rochester came to me, full of plans. He had written his banker for

jewelry that belonged to his family.

"Oh, sir," I said. "Never mind jewels. Jewels for Jane Eyre would be unnatural and strange. But there is something I have been wanting to ask you. Something I've been wondering about."

He looked disturbed. "What? Ask me anything, Jane," he said.

"Why did you take such pains to make me believe that you wanted to marry Miss Ingram? I don't understand."

"Is that all?" He smiled. "Why, I wished

to make you as madly in love with me as I was with you."

"Excellent!" I said. "But it was shameful to act in that way. Did you think nothing of Miss Ingram's feelings, sir?"

"Her only feeling is pride," he said. "When I started a rumor that my fortune was a fraction of its real worth, she showed me nothing but coldness. Now go and put on your bonnet, dear Jane. I want to take you into town with me."

Our errand in town was difficult. Mr. Rochester wanted me to choose silk for half a dozen dresses. When I brought the number down to two, he insisted on bright colors. With great trouble, I finally got him to agree to a black satin and a pearl-gray silk. "I will not be your English Céline Varens," I told him.

As we rode home in the carriage, I remembered the letter from my uncle. "It would be a relief if my uncle wished to give me a small amount of money," I thought to myself. "Then I could bear this golden shower of gifts from Mr. Rochester." That very day I wrote to my uncle in Madeira, telling him I would soon be married.

The days of courtship flew by. At last, just two days remained before the wedding. That night, I dreamed that Thornfield Hall was a ruin. Bats and owls were the only beings who lived there. When I woke, I thought it was day, for the room was light. But the light was from a candle. A stranger was in my room, a woman I had never seen before. She took my wedding veil from the closet, put it over her head and looked in the mirror. Her face was savage, with red eyes and dark, swollen lips. Taking the veil from her head, she ripped it in two. Then she came to my bed and held the candle close to my face. I fainted from terror.

The next day, I told Mr. Rochester what had happened. He said, "That was part dream, part reality. The woman must have been Grace Poole. I know you wonder why I keep such a woman in the house. When we have been married a year and a day, I will tell you. Does that satisfy you, Jane?"

In truth, I thought this must be the only explanation for what I had seen. When Mr.

Rochester asked me to spend the following night in Adèle's room, I was quite happy to accept.

The next morning, Mr. Rochester was in a great hurry to get to the church. As we entered, the clergyman, Mr. Wood, waited at the altar. The only other people in the church were two men who had slipped in by the side door.

The ceremony began. Soon Mr. Wood came to the passage, "If anyone here knows of any reason why this marriage cannot lawfully take place, he must now speak out."

Mr. Wood paused, which is the custom. But when is the pause after that sentence ever broken by a reply? Perhaps once in a hundred years. But when Mr. Wood opened his mouth to go on, a voice called out, "This marriage cannot take place!"

Mr. Wood looked at Mr. Rochester. Mr. Rochester clutched my arm unsteadily, as if an earthquake had rolled under his feet. But he said to the clergyman, "Go on."

The speaker came up to the altar. "I say the wedding cannot take place," he said.

"Mr. Rochester has a wife still living."

I stared at Mr. Rochester until he looked at me. His eyes were spark and flint.

"My name is Biggs," the stranger said firmly. "I am a lawyer from London. I have a document here stating that 15 years ago, Edward Rochester was married to Bertha Antoinetta Mason in Spanish Town, Jamaica. I also have a witness who can prove that Mr. Rochester's wife is still alive."

Mr. Mason stepped forward, afraid to meet Mr. Rochester's furious look.

"Impossible!" Mr. Wood cried. "I have lived in this district a great many years. I have never heard of a Mrs. Rochester at Thornfield Hall."

"Enough!" said Mr. Rochester. "I invite all of you to come up to the house and visit *my wife!*"

# Alone in the World

Mr. Rochester led us back to the house. Mrs. Fairfax, Leah, Adèle, and Sophie happily rushed out to greet us.

"Away with your congratulations!" said Mr. Rochester. "They are 15 years too late."

Holding my hand tightly, Mr. Rochester took us up to the room where Mr. Mason had been attacked.

Lifting the tapestry, he unlocked the secret door. Just inside, Grace Poole was cooking something over the fire. At the back of the room, a strange figure seemed to be moving around on all fours.

"Good-morrow, Mrs. Poole," said Mr. Rochester. "How are you? And how is your charge today?"

"We're well," said Grace.

Suddenly the figure gave a fierce cry.

"Ah, sir, she has seen you!" Grace said. "You'd better not stay."

The maniac roared again. Then she pulled her shaggy hair away from her swollen face. I knew her! This was the woman who had come to my room two nights before. Now she came toward us.

"Beware!" Grace screamed. At that, Biggs, Mason, and Wood stepped back. Mr. Rochester flung me behind him just as the demented creature sprang for his throat. She had her teeth against his cheek. They struggled. He could have stopped her with a single blow—but he would not. At last he was able to tie her to a chair.

Mr. Rochester turned to the men with a desolate smile. "That is *my wife*. And *this* is what I wished to have," he said, putting his hand on my shoulder. Judge me, if you will! Now, be off! I must shut up my prize."

Mr. Biggs turned to me. "Madame, you are clear of all blame in this matter. Your good uncle will be glad to hear it."

"My uncle? From Madeira?"

"Mr. Mason was in Madeira," Mr. Briggs

said. "He happened to be with Mr. Eyre when he learned of your coming marriage. Sadly, your uncle is very ill, too ill to travel. So he begged Mr. Mason to come to England to free you from the snare you had fallen into. I am only thankful we are not too late. Surely *you* must be thankful, too!"

I returned to my room alone. Jane Eyre, who had only this morning been a hopeful, passionate woman, was now a cold, solitary girl again. I thought of my love lost, my hope crushed, my faith death-struck. These thoughts swam full and mighty around me in one dark mass. The bitterness of the hours I passed cannot be described.

At last I left the room. Mr. Rochester was sitting in a chair across from my door. "I have been waiting for you," he said. "Jane, can you listen to me now?"

"For hours, sir, if you wish."

"My father did not want to divide his property," he began. "He gave everything to Rowland, my older brother. As for me, I was to make my fortune by marrying into a wealthy family. My bride was to be Bertha

Mason, the boast of Spanish Town.

"I saw little of Bertha until we were married. Then I learned that her mother and brother were mad. They were locked away in an asylum. Richard Mason will probably go mad someday, too.

"After the marriage, I found my wife completely different than I. I could not pass a single hour with her in comfort. Over time, the poor, deranged woman became stupid and coarse—and finally, violent.

"At last I returned to England. I placed her in comfort and safety with Grace Poole. But I could call her my wife no longer. She is not truly my wife, nor I her husband. *You* shall yet be my wife, Jane. I am not married. I shall keep only to you as long as you and I shall live."

"Sir, your wife is *living*," I said. "If I lived with you, I should be your mistress. To say otherwise is false. I must leave Thornfield."

"Oh, Jane, this is bitter! This—this is wicked. It would not be wicked to love me." A wild look of suffering was on his face.

"Wait, Jane!" he went on. "Give one

thought to the horror of my life when you are gone. Who can I turn to?"

I shook, fearing for him. But I was firmly resolved.

"Trust in God and yourself," I said. "Believe in heaven. We must hope to meet again there."

"Jane!" he cried, stretching out his arms to me. Blinded by tears, I rushed past him and went back into my room.

Before dawn the next morning, I took my purse, which had 20 shillings in it. Then I stole quietly out of the house.

As I walked along the road, I sobbed wildly. I hated myself.

Presently a public coach came along. I asked the driver where he was going. He named a place a long way off, where Mr. Rochester had no connections. It would do. I gave the driver most of my money and the coach rolled away.

Two days later, the driver set me down at a place called Whitcross. I slept that night in the grass. The next two days I looked for work—any kind of work. There was none to be found. When my money was gone, I tried to sell my gloves and handkerchief for food. One kind man gave me a piece of the loaf of bread he was eating, but most people turned me away. I saw that people are suspicious of beggars, especially well-dressed ones.

I spent another night outdoors. It was cold and damp. The next day I wandered like a lost and starving dog. Without food or shelter I knew I would soon die. Yet I could not accept the prospect of death while I knew Mr. Rochester was still alive.

I struggled on into the evening, leaving the village behind. Far in the distance, a single light gleamed. I followed it to a house. Looking through the window, I saw two young, graceful women. They seemed to be ladies in every way. I could hear their voices clearly, and I soon learned that their names were Mary and Diana. They were waiting for their brother, St. John. With them was a servant, Hannah.

I knocked at the door. When Hannah opened it, I asked her if I might speak to the ladies of the house. Suspicious of a stranger, she told me to leave. I sank to the ground, unable to move another step.

"I can but die," I said to myself. "Let me await God's will in silence."

Then a voice behind me said, "All human beings must die. But not all must meet a premature death such as this."

The door opened wider and Hannah looked out. "Is it you, Mr. St. John?"

"Yes. Let me bring this woman inside."

They fed me a little bread and milk. I told them my name was Jane Elliott. "Where are you from?" St. John asked. "What on earth has happened to you?"

"Sir," I said, "let me speak tomorrow."

The warmth of the fire made me drowsy. Soon, I was taken upstairs. My wet clothes were taken from me and I was put to bed. I thanked God—and slept.

11 Tragedy and Triumph

It was several days before I could rise from my bed. At last, one morning when I was strong enough, I came down to the kitchen, where Hannah was baking. I learned from her that the family's name was Rivers. The sisters, Mary and Diana, were governesses. They had been allowed to return home because of the recent death of their father. Their brother, St. John, was a parson who lived a few miles away.

Soon, all three of them returned from a walk. Mary and Diana kindly asked me how I was, and urged me to eat. St. John watched silently and then said, "When you tell us your friends' names, we can write. Then they may bring you back home."

"I must plainly tell you I am without home or friends," I declared.

"Where did you live last?" he asked.

"The name of the place must be my secret," I said. "I can only tell you I am free of any blame. All I ask is that you let me stay until I can find work of some kind."

"Indeed, you *shall* stay here!" said Diana.

One morning, St. John came to me with an offer of work. Could I teach the village girls at a small school in nearby Morton?

I accepted the position, and thanked him with all my heart.

As the day of parting grew near, St. John received a letter. Their Uncle John had died.

Diana told me, "We have never met or even seen our uncle. But we knew he had made a fortune of 20,000 pounds. My father always hoped he would leave us a little, but he has given everything to another relation." John locked the letter in his desk, and no one spoke of it again.

In Morton, I found that only a few of the girls could read or write. Many were rough and ill-mannered. But others were docile and had a sincere wish to learn. I was grateful to have the work, and for the simple little house that I had been given to live in.

I thought of the life I might have had with Mr. Rochester. I could have now been living in luxury as his mistress. I knew I had made the right choice. Yet I also knew that no one would ever love me so again.

One day, St. John brought me a book of poetry, and stopped to look at a picture I had been working on. Next to the picture was a thin, blank sheet of paper. Something on it caught his eye. Without explanation, he tore a tiny piece from the paper and put it in his glove. Then he said goodbye.

The following night, St. John again came to visit. "I have a story to tell which has not yet ended," he said. "Come sit near the fire."

"Some 20 years ago," he began, "a poor curate fell in love with a rich man's daughter. When she married him, she was disowned by her family. Before two years had passed, the unlucky couple had died. They had a daughter, however, who was raised by a Mrs. Reed of Gateshead. From there, the girl was sent to Lowood School. Later she became the governess of the ward of a certain Mr. Rochester at Thornfield Hall."

"*Mr. Rivers!*" I interrupted in shock.

"Please let me go on," he said. "This Mr. Rochester wished to marry the governess. But at the altar she discovered he had a wife still living—although she was a lunatic. The governess disappeared, but it is now of great importance that she be found. Mr. Biggs, a solicitor, has written to me about her. Tell me, Jane—is this not an odd tale?"

"What of Mr. Rochester?" I cried. "How is he and where is he? Is he well?"

"I know nothing of Mr. Rochester. But since you do not ask me the name of the governess," he said with a twinkle in his eye, "I suppose I must tell you myself."

He showed me the scrap of paper he had taken yesterday. In my own handwriting I could read the words, *Jane Eyre*. Without thinking, I must have written my real name on the paper.

"You did not ask why Mr. Biggs wanted to see you," St. John went on. "But he wished to tell you that your uncle, Mr. Eyre of Madeira, is dead. He has left you all of his property—you are a very rich woman."

"I! Rich?"

"Oh, yes, quite rich. You have 20,000 pounds."

The news took my breath away. "Don't you think there is a mistake?" I gasped.

"No mistake at all," said St. John. "But I must be going now." He got up to leave.

"Stop one minute!" I cried. "It puzzles me to know why Mr. Biggs wrote to *you*."

He said, "Oh, I am a clergyman. We are often asked about odd matters."

"No, that does not satisfy me," I said.

St. John tried to put me off, but I insisted that he tell me more. At last he admitted, "My mother's maiden name was Eyre. Can you believe it, Jane? We are cousins."

I stared at him. It seemed I had a brother and sisters whom I could admire and love. This was wealth indeed! But I would not have my sisters penniless, slaving among strangers. Nor a brother toiling in far-off India. I would divide my inheritance among us. At first St. John and his sisters resisted, but finally they gave in to my wishes. In their own hearts, my cousins must have felt that dividing the property was fair and just. If they had been in my place, they would surely have done the same thing.

Near Christmas, all was settled. Diana and Mary left their jobs as governesses and returned to the family house. I left the school at Morton, although I promised to return once a week to teach. Mary, Diana, and I were joyful, passing our days reading and studying together. Only St. John did not change his plans. He was still determined to become a missionary.

One evening St. John and I were talking after everyone had gone to bed. The candle had almost died out. Moonlight filled the room. Suddenly I felt the thrill of a shock through my body. "Quiet!" I cried.

St. John said, "What did you hear?"

I had heard a voice cry—"Jane! Jane!" I had no idea where it had come from, but it was the voice of Edward Rochester.

"I am coming!" I cried. "Wait for me! Oh, yes, I will come!"

The next morning I left for Thornfield.

As the coach rumbled along, I told myself, "Mr. Rochester may be beyond the English Channel. Or if he is at Thornfield Hall, who is there with him? His wife? Then you shall have nothing to do with him."

Yet when the coach set me down at a nearby inn, how quickly I walked toward Thornfield! At last it came into view.

It was a blackened ruin.

What had happened to that stately mansion, and to those who had lived there? Heartsick, I returned to the inn, where the innkeeper told me everything.

"It was the lunatic," he said. "She got out of her room one night and set the place ablaze. Mr. Rochester got the servants safely outside, and then went back to save her. She was on the roof, waving her arms above the battlements. When he got up close to her, she yelled and leaped away. The next moment she lay smashed on the pavement."

"Good God!"

"You may well say so, ma'am. As for Mr. Rochester, when he came down the stairway, there was a great crash. He was taken out from the ruins, but sadly hurt. Stone-blind he is now, and one hand so crushed that Dr. Carter had to amputate it directly."

"Where does he now live?" I asked.

"At Ferndean, a manor house on a farm he has in a far corner of the district."

"If you can get me there before dark this day, I'll pay you twice your usual price."

I arrived at Ferndean just as it was turning dark. I knocked softly at the door. A servant, Mary, opened it. She stared at me as if she was seeing a ghost. She had a glass of water on a tray for Mr. Rochester.

"Give the tray to me," I whispered softly. "I will carry it in myself."

The tray shook. Water spilt from the glass as I entered the parlor. Mr. Rochester's old dog Pilot jumped up as he saw me.

"Lie down, Pilot!" Mr. Rochester said.

I brought the water to him. Pilot followed after me, still excited.

"This is you, Mary, is it not?" Mr. Rochester asked uncertainly.

"Mary is in the kitchen," I said.

"*Who* is it, then? Great God, speak! What

a sweet madness has come over me!"

He groped in the air. I took his wandering hand and held it in mine.

"Such small, light fingers!" he said in disbelief. Then gathering me to him, he whispered, "Is it Jane? This is her shape."

"And this is her voice," I said. "Yes, she is all here. Her heart, too. From this day on, I will never leave your side."

"I did wrong, Jane," he said. "Had I kept you, I would have dirtied my innocent flower. Now I see the hand of God in my doom. Yet here I am, broken—a cripple. Am I hideous to look at, Jane?"

"*Very*, sir," I answered, "but you always were, you know."

"Hmmmph!" he replied. Yet blind as he was, a smile played over his face.

Reader, I married him. The first two years of our union, his blindness continued. Then, gradually, the sight returned to one of his eyes. One morning, when our firstborn child was placed in his arms, he could see that the boy had inherited his own eyes—large, brilliant, and black.